Cruella De Vil wanted lots of Dalmatian puppies – and she finished up with 99 of them! But why *did she want them? And why is this story called 101 Dalmatians?*

British Library Cataloguing in Publication Data
Disney, Walt
    Walt Disney's 101 Dalmatians.—(Ladybird Disney
    series. no. 845; 6)
    I. Title   II. Smith, Dodie. 101 Dalmatians
    813'.54[J]   PZ7
    ISBN 0-7214-0877-X

Walt Disney's
101 Dalmatians

Ladybird Books

Pongo the Dalmatian lived with a
young human called Roger
Radcliff, in a little flat which was
always untidy.

Then one day Roger got married.
His new wife was called Anita –
and *she* had a beautiful lady
Dalmatian called Perdita. Pongo
was pleased!

Everything went well until a friend
of Anita's called Cruella De Vil
came to visit them. Roger didn't
like her, and she frightened Perdita
and Pongo.

As she was leaving, Cruella looked
at the dogs and said, "Aren't their
coats beautiful! Do Dalmatians

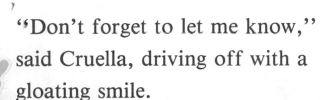

have lots of puppies? When are they expected?"

"She'll have six or seven," said Anita, "in three weeks' time."

"Don't forget to let me know," said Cruella, driving off with a gloating smile.

When at last Perdita's puppies were born, there weren't just six or seven. There were FIFTEEN! The humans, including Nanny the maid who looked after them, were delighted.

And as soon as they were all born,
Cruella turned up again.

"Fifteen!" she said, pleased. "I'll
buy all of them."

"Oh no, you won't," said Roger,
looking her straight in the eye.
"We're not selling a single one."

Cruella was furious, and slammed
the door as she left.

Pongo and Perdita were overjoyed
that all the puppies were going to
be kept. But they wouldn't have
been nearly so happy if they could
have seen Cruella at that moment.

"She was talking to Horace and
Jasper Badun, who were very nasty
crooks indeed. They were planning
to dognap all those puppies!

One night soon after this, the two
Baduns sat in their truck near the
house. They were waiting for
Roger and Anita to take Perdita
and Pongo for their walk.

12

13

When the four came out, the two
Baduns hurried over to the house.
Nanny the maid tried to stop them,
but they forced their way in.

They picked up all the puppies, and minutes later the truck was on its way.

Next day the story was in every newspaper. There were pictures of Perdita and Pongo, and Anita and Roger. The police got busy and there were even Scotland Yard detectives hunting for the puppies.

But days went by, and no one found them.

At last Pongo said to Perdita, "It's no good. The humans aren't getting anywhere. We'll have to find the puppies ourselves."

"How can we do that?" asked Perdita, weeping. "We don't even know where to start."

"We'll try the Twilight Bark," said Pongo. "It's the quickest way to send and get news."

By the time the two Dalmatians
were taken for their walk that day,
it was almost dark. When they got
to the top of Primrose Hill, Pongo
barked the alert – three loud barks
and a howl.

They waited a moment, then an answering bark was heard. "It's the Great Dane over at Hampstead!" said Pongo, and he barked out his message.

Danny the Great Dane was very surprised at the message. "Fifteen puppies have been stolen!" he told a terrier friend. "They're Dalmatians. The humans haven't been able to find them, so it's up to us to send out an all-dog alert with the Twilight Bark."

And his big deep voice began to send the news all over London.

Two mongrels heard the alert. One said, "I bet those puppies are a long way away by now. I think we should let the rest of the country know."

"Good thinking!" said his friend. "I'll go to the railway station and pass the word. You go down and tell the river dogs."

Within the hour, word had spread north, south, east and west – all over England.

It wasn't long before the barking was heard by an old army horse called Captain. "Sounds like an alert!" he said to the cat who was lying on his back. "Sergeant Tibs, get Colonel at once."

Colonel was a gruff old sheepdog,
and he was sleeping in the hayloft.
When he had listened to the
barking, he told the others about
the message. Fifteen stolen
puppies!

"That's funny," said Sergeant Tibs. "I heard puppies barking over at the old De Vil house last night."

"No one lives there now," said Colonel. "Let's go and see."

The three of them went quietly up
to a broken window and peered
through. The first thing they saw
was a television set. Two crooks –
the Baduns – were watching it. And
all round the room there were
puppies. Not fifteen – nor even
fifty – but *ninety nine* of them!

From dog to dog, all the way back
to London, went the news that the
puppies had been found. At last it
reached Dan, the Great Dane at
Hampstead.

From him it went straight to Pongo and Perdita, and they wasted no time. They set off, going as fast as they could.

Meanwhile, Sergeant Tibs was keeping watch on the De Vil house. He saw Cruella drive up to the door, and he went to the window to hear what was happening.

She was saying to the Baduns, "I
want the skins of all those puppies
for fur coats. Just see that they're
ready in the morning." And with
that, she slammed the door and
was gone.

Tibs was so horrified that he sat
and trembled for a whole minute.
Fur coats from puppy skins! What
a truly horrible thought!

There wasn't a moment to lose.
The Baduns were watching

television again. Tibs crept through the broken window and whispered to the nearest puppy, "Tell everyone they must escape. Cruella is after your hides!"

One by one the puppies crawled quietly out of the room. Then Tibs took them upstairs to hide under a bed.

At that moment Colonel, the old
sheepdog, heard Pongo barking at
the nearby crossroads. He barked
back, telling the Dalmatian how to
get to the De Vil house.

But now the Baduns had
discovered that the puppies had
gone. They were hunting for them.

So when the two Dalmatians
arrived minutes later, they found
the puppies backed into a corner of
the bedroom. Tibs was in front
trying desperately to protect them
from the Baduns.

Pongo and Perdita bounded into
action. Pongo went for Jasper
Badun, and Perdita pulled the rug
from under Horace.

Under cover of the fight, Tibs led
the puppies out of the house and
along to the stable.

When they had finished with the Baduns, Pongo and Perdita dashed after the puppies. "Are all fifteen here?" asked Perdita anxiously.

It was the old horse, Captain, who answered. "Fifteen and a few more," he said. "There are ninety nine."

"*Ninety nine*!" said Pongo, astonished. "Whatever did Cruella want with ninety nine puppies?"

There was silence for a moment, then a puppy said, "She was going to make fur coats out of us."

Perdita and Pongo looked at each other. They had never dreamed of anything so evil.

"We'll just have to take them back to London," said Perdita. "Roger and Anita won't turn them out."

As they set out across the snow on
their way back to London, Perdita
was worried again. There were so
many puppies that their pawprints
could be seen very easily.

And they were! Cruella in her car,
and the Baduns in their truck, were
soon after them.

Only one thing would help: disguise. The puppies all rolled in some soot until they looked like black Labradors, then they climbed into a van which was going straight to London.

Then some real luck came along. The Baduns' truck crashed into Cruella's car – and they were both out of action!

Home at last, and Anita, Roger and Nanny started to clean off the soot. Then Nanny said, "Have you noticed that there seem to be a lot *more* of them?"

Roger started to count. "Fourteen under the Christmas tree – sixty two – ninety four – and five

over there makes ninety nine.
That's a hundred and one
Dalmatians counting Perdita
and Pongo!''

''Whatever are we going to do
with them all?'' asked Anita.

''Do?'' said Roger. ''Why, we'll
keep them all, of course.''